the other Ark

ARK 2

Lynley Dodd

It rained
and it rained,
it BUCKETED down,
teeming in torrents
on mountain
and town.

Noah was ready.
He looked at the mud.
'No time to lose,' he said,
'here comes the
Flood!
I really must hurry
before it gets dark,
to load all these animals
into the
Ark.'
Shipshape and steady,
on skittering toes,
they filed up the gangplank
in well-behaved
rows.

'ENOUGH!'
thundered Noah.
He bolted the door.
'This Ark is JAM PACKED!'
he said,
but . . .
there were more.
He studied the view
of the animal queue
and called to a friend of his,
Sam Jam Balu.
'Sam,' he said kindly,
'you've nothing to do
and I really need help
with this two-by-two zoo.
My problems are solved
if you're quick off the mark –
you can take all the rest
in my second-best Ark.'

He pulled up the gangplank
with no more delay,
he hoisted the anchor
and sailed
far away.

'This task is a doddle,'
said Sam Jam Balu,
as he started to gather
HIS load,
two by two.
'I'm A1 efficient,
I KNOW what to do –
there's nothing too tricky
for Sam Jam Balu.'

There were hip-hopping hippos

and burrowing flumps,
candy-striped camels
with comical humps.

Armory dilloes
and carnival cats,
mad kangaroosters
in bow ties and spats.

'I'm A1 efficient,
I KNOW what to do –
there's nothing too tricky,'
said Sam Jam Balu.

There were flying flapdoodles
and butternut bears
with polka-dot piffles
in quarrelsome pairs.

Blunderbuss dragons,
Mongolian sneeth
and alligatigers
with too many teeth.

'I'm A1 efficient,
I KNOW what to do –
there's nothing too tricky,'
said Sam Jam Balu.

There were dithering dingbats
and elephant snails,
pom-pom palavers
with curlicue tails.

Marmalade mammoths
and sabre-tooth mice,
dirty old dinosaurs,
(not very nice).

'This task is a doddle,'
said Sam Jam Balu,
as he pushed and he pulled
and he puffed
and he blew.
'I'm A1 efficient,
I KNOW what to do –
there's nothing too tricky
for Sam Jam Balu.'

He pulled up the gangplank
at noon on the dot,
he hoisted the anchor
and . . .
STUCK
TO
THE
SPOT.

Books by Lynley Dodd

HAIRY MACLARY FROM DONALDSON'S DAIRY
HAIRY MACLARY'S BONE
HAIRY MACLARY'S CATERWAUL CAPER
HAIRY MACLARY'S RUMPUS AT THE VET
HAIRY MACLARY SCATTERCAT
HAIRY MACLARY'S SHOWBUSINESS
HAIRY MACLARY, SIT
HAIRY MACLARY AND ZACHARY QUACK
HAIRY MACLARY AND FRIENDS: FIVE MORE LYNLEY DODD STORIES
HAIRY MACLARY: FIVE LYNLEY DODD STORIES

A DRAGON IN A WAGON
FIND ME A TIGER
HEDGEHOG HOWDEDO
THE MINISTER'S CAT ABC
MY CAT LIKES TO HIDE IN BOXES *(with Eve Sutton)*
SCARFACE CLAW
SCHNITZEL VON KRUMM'S BASKETWORK
SCHNITZEL VON KRUMM, DOGS NEVER CLIMB TREES
SCHNITZEL VON KRUMM FORGET-ME-NOT
SLINKY MALINKI
SLINKY MALINKI CATFLAPS
SLINKY MALINKI, OPEN THE DOOR
SNIFF-SNUFF-SNAP!
WAKE UP, BEAR

PUFFIN BOOKS
Published by the Penguin Group: London, New York, Ireland, Australia, Canada, India, New Zealand and South Africa
Penguin Books Ltd, Registered Offices: 80 Strand, London WC2R 0RL, England

www.penguin.com

First published in New Zealand by Mallinson Rendel Publishers Ltd 2004
Published in Great Britain in hardback in Puffin Books 2005
Published in paperback 2006
3 5 7 9 10 8 6 4
Copyright © Lynley Dodd, 2004
All rights reserved
The moral right of the author/illustrator has been asserted
Made and printed in China
ISBN–13: 978–0–14150–018–8
ISBN–10: 0–141–50018–2